Tales by Erin

EA Harwik

Published by EA Harwik, 2022.

TALES BY ERIN

First edition. November 21, 2022.

Copyright © 2022 EA Harwik.

ISBN: 979-8215487181

Written by EA Harwik.

Table of Contents

.... 1

Table of Contents 2

About the Author 3

Miss Fruitcake's Apple Blossom 4

Caveman 10

A C4 on the BW 12

Growing Pains 23

A Passing Moment 27

A Further Moment 28

A Precious Moment 32

Warrior Chick 43

The Last Page 58

Tales by Erin

A collection of short stories

by EA Harwik

Miss Fruitcake's Apple Blossom

MY JOURNEY BEGAN ON the 19th of April 2004. Our social science teacher arranged for the class to visit a local nursing home. We'd talk to interested residents about their experiences so we could produce an essay as an assignment for class. Our teacher felt everyone might benefit from the outing. The residents could enjoy our company, and we'd gain from their experiences. Plus it would enhance our intuitive writing skills.

The nursing home public relations officer read from a list and allocated me to Dulcie. I asked for Dulcie's full name, thinking it rather disrespectful for an unknown teenager to address a senior citizen by her given name. I was told her name was Dulcie Jones—Miss Jones. And with the aid of a spiteful-looking screwed-up face the PR lady added, "We call her Miss Fruitcake around here. She's 103 years old and lives in the dementia ward, so she won't care what you call her."

This was just what I needed to feel really confident about the whole venture. I've never been one to warm to old people. They all seem to want to pull at my cheek while saying, "My, look how you've grown".

In a manner seeming best suited to the military or infant school, we were herded through corridors and strategically married to a name-labelled door via a clipboard pen stroke then left, without explanation, to venture forward alone.

The lady in *my* room was on her bed semi-dozing, so I waited quietly until she sensed my presence and stirred, before introducing myself and explaining why I was here. To my surprise, Miss Jones sat up while colour entered her face to complement the glow of a thousand smiles. I'd expected an immobile wretched old hag lying mouth open with a blank stare, and a proven capacity to think of nothing at all for prolonged periods.

Miss Jones took me to her terrace, where we sat with a view across the duck pond. Her walk was somewhat slow. She used a cane for balance but was clearly a lady of personal pride who valued independence. We started getting to know each other with small talk mostly about ducks. They had come to greet her when she appeared. We fed them bread. I was impressed how Miss Jones had labelled every duck with a symbolic name. And how she was able to control their greed via skilful management. She explained with a laugh how difficult it had been to teach *Gluten* to fake manners and gain advantage by refraining from bullying the others by pecking.

Miss Jones's speech wasn't fragmented or vague, as I'd expected. She had the gift of an interesting storyteller. I was amazed by her passionate descriptions, captivating tone and faint yet gorgeously European accent.

We chatted a little of nothing and everything, exchanging questions for answers about life. She knew more about the pressures of being a teen today than my own parents could ever explain or understand. Miss Jones obviously followed world events with a keen interest and was willing to express any view she arrived at through logical thought. Quite refreshing as most of the *grown-ups* I know have no view of their own. They blindly follow what best suits their current prejudice.

I explained the music I liked, and she actually knew whom I was talking about but added that I would never win her over. The Viennese waltz together with the old classical masters had closed her brain forever. She had no vacant room in her heart to fall in love with new musicians or music.

Eventually we talked about a rich, long, tragic and interesting tale titled *her life.*

Miss Jones was born on the 5th June 1901 in Peterhof, Russia. During her life, she had changed her name many times. Her birth name was Anastasia Romanov. Her mother had also changed names, having been born Victoria Alix Helena Louise Beatrix but later becoming Alexandra Feodorovna when her mother became *Her Imperial Majesty, Tsarina of all the Russias.* Her father was *His Imperial Majesty Nicholas II, Tsar, Emperor, and All-Russian Autocrat.*

Until the age of fifteen, Anastasia lived with her parents, three older sisters and younger brother in luxury beyond the richest dreams of all but the royal families of Europe. The family reign was abruptly ceased in 1916 by a people's revolution. For two years, the family was held under house arrest in the Ural

Mountains of Siberia, at Yekaterinburg. On the 17th July 1918, the whole family, together with some family aides, were lined up against a basement wall and shot. Without knowing how or why, Anastasia was able to live through the carnage. She was pulled from the pile of bleeding bodies, rushed away and hidden in exile. Miss Jones didn't know whether any of her siblings had also survived and escaped. She was very sure her mother and father were both dead. They had pleaded loudly to spare their children and stood in front of them. Only a parent would understand.

From 1919 until 1938 she lived as Agathe Genevieve in France on a prosperous farm on the outskirts of Nancy. To be inconspicuous, she was employed in domestic service by a modestly wealthy family. Her only link to the past was to be via someone called Boris who would explain they were *the keepers of dreams* in their introduction. Boris was to appear in times of need to make arrangements.

With the threat of war imminent, Boris materialized and Agathe was whisked away to England where she became Dorothy Middlemiss, an employee for a family bakery, in Surrey. Upon the outbreak of the second European War Dorothy became an interpreter for the Home Office. A position she held until 1948, when a journalist stopped her in the street, asking questions about her past. But a man she'd never seen before interrupted the journalist and introduced himself as Boris, *the keeper of dreams.* Within 24 hours Dorothy was on a steamer bound for the United States carrying papers identifying her as Mrs Stacey Grant, a war widow.

Stacey settled in Ellicott City, Maryland. She opened a modest guesthouse, which over the years provided a comfortable existence. Her past seemed a distant memory. Mrs Grant became accepted as a long-standing and popular local resident.

In 1987, aged 86, Stacey was planning to retire. She longed to sell her well-patronized and valuable guesthouse to commence a less hectic lifestyle in a small cottage somewhere quiet. But a nightmare suddenly erupted when the guesthouse was besieged by reporters. Ellicott City's conservative and ever-reliable Mrs Grant was exposed on national television as a long-missing Russian Princess.

A stranger broke into her locked house and introduced himself as *the keeper of dreams.* Boris arranged a comical distraction and drove Stacey to Andrews air force base, where she boarded a waiting military aircraft and was flown to Los Angeles International Airport.

Miss Dulcie Jones, a retired schoolteacher, emerged and boarded the waiting Pan Am, non-stop flight to Sydney, Australia. A connecting flight and taxi ride completed the transition to a modest cottage on the outskirts of Canberra.

In 2002, aged one hundred and one, Miss Jones sold her home and became a resident of the room in the nursing home where we sit today.

Miss Jones stopped talking and sat in silence waiting for my response. I was speechless for some time. I tried to say something four times but stopped to reword my question. Eventually I was able to ask, "Is this why the nursing staff calls you Miss Fruitcake?"

Miss Jones replied, "Of course it is. I kept my secret safe for so long by stealth and deception. And now finally I'm free. No one believes the word of an old lady in a nursing home."

"May I visit you again, Miss Jones? Today has been fun. You're easy to talk to. It's great sharing ideas with you." I could see the public relations officer and my teacher searching for a missing mark on their clipboard aboard an already loaded bus, bar one. Miss Jones smiled and said she would be delighted to receive me.

I left somewhat quieter and more introspective than how I'd arrived.

On the way back to school and during the next few lessons, I listened to my classmates exchange *comical* stories about boring old fuddy-duddies who were guilty of a wasted life. The consensus was that most should have been lined up against a wall and shot to save them and the community further burden.

I wrote a story for my school assignment. I described in detail how Miss Jones devoted her life to teaching children. How she became head teacher at Cootamundra primary school, where she taught for forty-three years. The story described how Miss Jones had retired to the outskirts of Canberra to live alone, save for an overweight, bossy tabby cat named Boris. In the story, Miss Jones spent her last days pondering lost opportunities consumed in regret. I received an A+ for my work. I showed Miss Jones. She laughed and even offered storyline improvements.

I wrote another story about a beautiful young Russian Princess who was forced to journey the world in an attempt to maintain her safety and privacy. I explained how the Princess regretted nothing and smiled as she slept each night on the strength of fulfilling dreams. I kept this story secret sharing it only with Miss Jones who shed a small tear as she read. She showed me a letter she'd received in 2003 from a solicitor's office. The letter was to inform her Uncle Boris had passed away and she alone was now *the keeper of dreams.* Boris left her his only possession. A key to a safety deposit-box in a Canberra bank where it was explained the dream was stored.

In July, during a regular visit to my new friend and confidante, Miss Jones asked if I would retrieve the deposit-box contents. She wanted to see her planned destiny one last time. I was a little puzzled but knew I could trust Miss Jones. I took the next afternoon off school using the excuse explained in a note I wrote so it appeared to be from my father. Key in hand, I visited the bank, signed some papers and retrieved a wooden *shoe-box.* I placed the box in a Kmart shopping bag and delivered it to Miss Jones on my bicycle.

Miss Jones left the door to her room open so as not to attract attention. The box revealed a Fabergé Easter egg labelled, *The Apple Blossom.* It was truly magnificent. Miss Jones explained that when she left Russia, the three Fabergé Easter eggs manufactured in her birth year, 1901, had also been smuggled out to provide for her future.

The other two had been exchanged to secure her safety. One, the *Basket of Wildflowers* egg was given to Great Britain in exchange for safe passage in 1938. The egg was now a personal possession of her second cousin by marriage, Queen Elizabeth II. The other, the *Gatchina Palace* egg was given to the United States to secure her passage in 1948. The egg remained on display in Baltimore at the Walters art gallery.

Miss Jones asked me to care for the *Apple Blossom* egg and return it to the Russian people when she died. She explained it belonged to them and added, "You are my Boris now. You're *the keeper of dreams.*"

When I discovered the egg was valued at around four million dollars, I thought we should return it to the bank for safekeeping. Touching it was a life changing experience.

On the 14th July 2004, while visiting Miss Jones, she smiled, motioned a soft kiss, closed her eyes and died.

The nursing home administrator gave me a locket saying, "She wanted you to have this. Aside from her clothes this was her only possession." Adding through a lopsided expression, "She was such a fruitcake. It won't be valuable." The locket was opened and held for the benefit of my inspection. "It has an image of an old family. We think it's the Czar family. They must have lived in Cootamundra. She was a schoolteacher there. She never told a soul but we found out from someone who knew of one of her past students."

On the morning of The 17th July 2004, I retrieved the box in the Kmart bag and rode my bicycle to the Russian embassy. I asked the security guard manning the gate if I could return some personal property. I was eventually shown into an office. Several junior clerks almost fell over when the box was opened. I was eagerly ushered to the Ambassador's suite and introduced. I told him my name was Boris. I explained the Fabergé *Apple Blossom* egg was being returned under instruction from *Her Imperial Princess, Anastasia,* who had joined the rest of her family. It was her bequest to have the egg quietly returned to the Russian people. I'm not sure whether the ambassador believed me, but he gave me a receipt and shook my hand while offering an upright and formal silent nod that spoke of gratitude and respect.

In the afternoon I attended Miss Jones's funeral. The priest and I were the only people present. At the burial, two gravediggers working further along the cemetery must have felt my loneliness. They came to the graveside and stood beside me. The priest quickly did the necessary for a *nobody* funeral and rushed off without offering a further word. One of the gravediggers asked who she was. I thanked them for attending and through sadness and pride explained, "She was my princess."

Caveman

FOR THREE DAYS SHE had taken an evening stroll through the grassy area winding among the palm trees, *bathing* in the cool autumn freshness. Her demeanour overflowed with a calm joy taking advantage of newly acquired freedom to stimulate her skin with the fresh taste of contentment. Recently blossomed maturity was pulsing like a beacon through smooth, pure, firm, budding curves.

He had noticed her wandering the palm garden. It was impossible for him to ignore her. He had tried to intersect with her the night before, but she had kept moving and it was as if his presence had gone unnoticed. *Tonight would be different.* As the evening cooled with the first hint of dew across the grass, he had selected his favoured club and was now sitting quietly between the golden cane and a large cycad.

Sure enough, with the distant flicker of a television set indicating the commencement of Law and Order SVU, she made her appearance. Slowly at first, cautiously following a safe path with a clear view to each side. There was hesitation in her movement not seen before. As if alarm bells were sounding a warning. Yet with time, she settled, confidence entered her movement as she wandered further towards the open space where the scent of evening freshness was strongest.

She had passed the Alexandra palm and was making her way towards a clump of flowers, obviously drawn towards their inviting perfume. He jumped to his feet and ran forward with his club extended, executing a sweeping strike that caught her. She tumbled to the ground on her left side. Appearing dazed and confused she instinctively rolled onto her tummy and lifted. Again he struck with a heavy direct blow to her back. She fell to the ground, stunned, and took two further blows. The third heavy timed strike gave off a crack. She quivered momentarily before stillness entered her limbs. He had shattered her spine.

He painted his face in victory and paused to gloat before rolling her onto her back. The pure lines of her post-adolescent form still offering both succulent youth and maturity. Teary helpless eyes stared up with defenceless pity etched across his reflection.

He pushed his club to her throat, crushing her windpipe and watched without feeling as she struggled to find air. Eventually her soft body fell limp. The last of her young life had melted away. Without hesitating, he put down his club and carried her lifeless body to a waiting pit, where he dropped her to rot with the compost.

He walked to the house, placed his club by the sliding door and slumped to a chair in front of the television. His wife poured him a beer uttering, "So you got her."

He took a large swig and through a confident stare said, "Her DNA has been extinguished. The only good cane toad is a dead cane toad."

A C4 on the BW

AT THE RISK OF SOUNDING like a complete whinger, I'll start by saying I'm a disappointment. My life sucks. All I ever do is dream and plan how to survive a future of doing nothing.

However, had we met eighty-seven days ago, I would have told you life was great, my future was sound, my expectations were high, and my dreams were on-track. That would be the eighty-seven days ago before I drove into town to pick up takeaway. Before I was slammed by an SUV, which resulted in my being pasted all over by six family-size meat-lover pizzas. I also received numerous bruises and a C4 spinal injury.

I don't remember much about the time immediately following the accident. I'm told it took three days to remove the meat lover smell from the hospital room. My dog, Gus would have loved to sleep on the bed under those conditions, but he was banned. It took a further sixteen days for me to figure that as a C4 spinal patient, I'm supposed to feel lucky if I can waggle my head. Apparently, I have no excuse if I don't spend my time smiling at everyone. All the other patients in the spinal ward have learned to make the staff feel better by explaining loudly and often how lucky they feel. Though my injuries are different somehow. I can't find my way clear to share in the joy of the occasion.

It takes quite a lot of adjusting to, not being able to move anything below your shoulders. Bathroom duties and general hygiene are a tad humiliating, not only because someone does the cleaning work on you, but also because you don't have any control over what they are doing or what you have done. Being fed by a *helper,* who always wants you to eat a few more spoonfuls of everything makes one feel so *adult.* It fosters a quick understanding of why children choose to spit food back at the feeder. When reality bites and the ongoing lack of dignity or purpose start to grind, breaking you in tears, you suffer a further indignity. Not being able to place your face in your hands to cry is quite a new unpleasant experience.

I truly loved how the *administration problems* were worked through so I could prepare for home to *pick up my life*. Administration consisted of the medical team and my parents discussing at length, in front of me, my requirements and setting a time to effect the changes. They started with house, room locations, lifting aids, etc, how to prevent me from choking to death if I need to cough. Moving quickly along, we came to the need for a colostomy bag, which they titled *our little ongoing problem*. The sintering of my spine for *good posture,* meaning they can sit me in the corner more easily. Of course, they had the inevitable discussion about menstruation, which was referred to as *the lady problem.* The doctor and the welfare sociologist exchanged ideas with my mother, explaining that sterilization would give the best outcome. Mother was not completely convinced. She seemed to think I'm still going to chance upon some prince charming, marry and have beautiful babies. They skipped any talk of future mobility. I guess mother didn't want them to upset me, and besides, she assured them she would be taking good care of me. I would want for nothing.

Not once during this *administration* discussion was I asked, spoken to or even given a quick glance. "Welcome to life on the ranch," is all I can think. Although it wouldn't be all bad as mother loves moving her prized pot plants around the house to keep them at their best so clearly she will eagerly do the same to me. Besides she had been trying to have me appear more ladylike for years. Now she can throw away my dungarees, dress me up in whatever she wants and there will not be a damn thing I can do about it. "Poor me." Mother agreed to give *the lady problem* a trial, acknowledging if it became too much she would bring me back to have things improved.

SO HERE I AM. THE BIG day has arrived. We have said our goodbyes and best wishes for the future. I have even had some good luck and a few blessings bestowed upon me as I am transferred to a smaller more manageable bed for the journey out of the spinal ward into my future.

The ambulance drives past the white fenced home paddocks of the family ranch, the BW. Sure enough as the ambulance door opens, mother is there all excited about having her loving twenty-two-year-old daughter home. The ambulance officers skilfully wheel and manhandle me into the house to my new room, which had been a formal dining room in a past life. I'm to be near the kitchen so Mother and I can have fun bonding.

I guessed correctly. The room is freshly painted girlie pink with all the expected trim. The bed is ever so sweet with at least a dozen pillows each adorned by coloured satin ribbons and delicate lace. Strangely the room has no TV. In the hospital I'd become something of a daytime soap junky. It was as if I couldn't drag myself away. Sorry, I guess that was my sick joke. I asked Mother about a TV and got the response, "Oh we won't have time for TV. We will be far too busy." God, I think, but say nothing. I practise my best diplomatic smile. It is only then that I notice how an ornate French partition is hiding all those ugly lifting thing-a-me-things that must clearly be distressing to Mother's eyes and will therefore be restricted to minimal usage.

"Now, I'll just leave you with these nice men so they can put you in bed, and I'll be back directly with a nice cup of tea for us," Mother says as she hurries to the kitchen rendering herself busy to the task of tea and pumpkin scones. The ambulance guys place me in bed, decline the cup of tea and with a well-positioned wink for my eyes only make a polite escape. While I start the first of probably six daily cuppas for the rest of my life. I'm not sure whether it even registers with Mother that I never drink tea.

Mother commenced to explain how tomorrow we will be busy as several of the ladies' institute auxiliary committee members are coming over to discuss strategies for next month's fundraiser to buy the priest's new robes. All the while, Mother keeps putting the cup to my mouth, allowing me to take another sip and goes on, and on, about gold thread, plush bone chiffon material, white trim and …

~~zzz~~

The sunset is that red reserved for the clearest summer days, soaked with ribbons of blue and purple that seem to shimmy the light as it fades into darkness.

I dismount, tether Jess to the fence, finger rub a few aches from my rear and stretch my back. I pull on my chaps to get them away from my crutch and stroll towards the fire, take a quick scupper of coffee to wash down the dust. Satisfied with the coffee, I stroll over to the cattle trough, remove my hat and dunk my head to clean up, or cool down. I'm not sure which. I let the cool water run down my shirt as I stand up and finger my hair back before replacing my hat. I park on an upturned bucket near the camp kitchen, take another few swigs of coffee and listen to the herd tally.

Eventually Soc comes out with, "Three hundred and twenty-six heads. Not a bad day's work. I reckon Joe and Mullet can do another sweep through the canyon come first light, to pick up any stragglers. That will just about do the roundup. Buck and Stretch. You guys can take to the branding and culling at the corral on your own until Joe and Mullet are through. And, I'll have a nice lie-in with a silver-service breakfast." He stops talking to grin through clenched teeth. "I reckon we have two more days ahead of us out here. Hope the weather holds. The sunset seems to be saying so. Hey, cookie, where in hell's the grub? A man could go grey waiting for a feed around here. Jesus Joe! I wouldn't be getting too settled on that bucket. It's got a rattler under it. I didn't want to shoot the damn thing with all the cattle so close."

My heart rate jumps into overdrive as I spring to my feet, spilling coffee everywhere. I quickly put in a few yards between the bucket and myself without a thought while the guys provide rapturous applause...

~~zzz~~

"Dear, dear! Joanne dear, can you hear me?"

I wake from a delightful mini-sleep to witness Mother standing over me with a somewhat whitish complexion. She has the first-aid kit in her hand. I'm not sure what she's about to do. I'm not sure she knows what she is about to do. Clearly she must have thought I'd died.

"Oh, there you are my dear, you did give me a start. You must be tired from your trip. I'll let you have a little nap to build up your strength before lunch. I'll be just next door in the kitchen if you need me," Mother says, as she pulls two blankets up to my chin, aligns some loose hairs on my head, kisses me on the cheek and shuffles off into her joining dominion.

I go back to sleep, but the joy of being at work on the ranch doesn't return. Those dreams are my special treats. They don't happen every day. It's such a joy to be able to *live* outside this room, this body.

I have no idea how long I slept. It couldn't have been long but I wake with a splitting headache. A sure sign I'm overheating. Before I can concentrate on how to try and explain to mother to uncover me, I become aware of muffled sounds and Mother issuing instructions. I open my eyes to be confronted with the five males of my life lined up like scarecrows on a wire. Each is dressed to the nines in Saturday night heel-kicking clobber. Save for one, all are wearing only socks, clean socks. Obviously mother made the boots stay on the veranda, no matter how clean they might have been. The fifth male, my best mate Gus, is in bare feet. He's clearly been worked over a treat with cleaning apparatus to gain passage into the house. He is sitting up on the floor with a pantingly irresistible smile on his face. He even has a red scarf around his neck like a pooncey town dog might wear on a Sunday stroll through the park. I would give anything to put my arms around his neck. I give out a "Gus, here boy!" with a wish I could hit the bed to encourage him. I watch as in one leap he jumps onto the bed. He immediately pulls the blankets away with his mouth and lays beside me, his head on my shoulder. He looks up to gain my approval, which he receives.

Although she said nothing, Mother must have aged three years to have Gus lying in bed with me on her finery.

Soc -—sorry, Bill, my father -—spoke saying, "That'd be right. We spend two days and a gallon of shampoo plus a tube of toothpaste getting that *flee bag* cleaned up. We had to work shifts last night to stop him rolling in anything disgusting, only to have him take over in here and get all the attention."

We're banned from calling Father Soc within earshot of the house. Mother has never approved of gross *cattle sale yard* talk and behaviour.

Buck, Mullet and Stretch came closer to check me out. I can see they're all itching to make a crack about my being dressed in a nightie with pink flowers and frills all over it. But can't find an appropriate way to broach the topic in front of Mother. Stretch *broke the ice* saying, "Joe. I was wondering how long it was going to take for you to go to town and back. When do we get our pizza?"

Mother's complexion takes on an alarming colour. She turns to Father. "That's enough! You can all go back to the barn until you learn how to behave in polite society. I would have thought you should know better by now, William Whitman."

Soc, sorry Bill, backs off a few steps before saying, "That's right boys. Stretch, you'd better hop it back to the barn while I decide if I'm going to dock you a month's pay or sack you outright for that outburst. I reckon you all belong in the barn. Mullet, pick that dog off of her and take him outside before he farts in that fancy sack. Buck, grab her and take her down to the barn as well. She needs to learn not to laugh at Stretch's terrible jokes. Stretch, you'd better make yourself useful. Follow Buck and make sure she doesn't turn blue, purple or green on the way, but don't go getting any ideas. Don't be staring at her flower covered butt, right."

With that, everything took on a new perspective. Buck grabs me around the hips and throws me over his shoulder like a bag of spuds. All I see is the ground with my own arms dangling in front of me. And, they are swaying; a pleasant sight indeed.

Mother's voice gets further away. She is going on about my being sick and how this is no way to treat me. And, don't get me dirty or smelly. I hear Soc reply, "She's not sick; she's over all that. Our daughter has a disability to live with now." There is a delay before he adds, "But she will be sick if you leave her lying in that bed all day." There is another delay while Soc takes a deep breath. "Now if you don't mind, we have cattle to tend to. I'll take my lecture tonight when I'm all washed up for the day."

As I bounce along on Buck's shoulder, Gus moves in between my arms and looks up at me while running his head across my outstretched fingers. He's having fun too.

I hear Soc say, "Okay, plonk her on those hay bails and get that clobber out we found. Whoever heard of a cowhand wearing pink flowers? Disgusting behaviour. What's the world coming to?"

No sooner has he finished speaking when down I go on a stack of hay. I find myself lounging in a purpose-fashioned seat made of hay bails with a cotton cover over it. They strip me down to my underwear and re-dress me in work shirt, jeans and boots. Stretch even goes to the trouble of buckling on my chaps and spurs before pulling gloves over my hands; it is great to feel human. I have a top view across the house yards from my perch. And for the first time in ages I can feel the breeze blow upon my face. This is no accident. These guys have been planning this stunt for some time.

Soc tells Buck to get in there and round up that there thingummy do-dad and get it moving this way. He adds, "And show Joe how to make the thing do as it's told."

In no time Buck returns with a funny looking control console. He places it around my neck before saying, "Pay attention, Joe, 'cause Soc sent me to Pennsylvania to learn how to work this thing. I'll explain but I know he is going to sack me if we mess it up. Okay?" I nod him a wink before he continues, "You blow and suck on these tubes, right. And watch the lights to get the functions right, right. Okay here we go. To call the thing to come you get that light to go. Good. Look! Here it comes." He waves an arm towards the barn.

I look up and can't believe my eyes. A funny looking thing has come out of the barn and is heading towards us. Buck continues, "This would be your iBot 3000 using the remote function. Gee! Blow there, get that light on and stop it before it starts making out on my leg. Okay, let's get you up and in the saddle."

He picks me up with his now familiar over the shoulder lift technique and places me in the iBot 3000 which unfolded, expanding into a chair by itself when I blow it to a stop.

Buck continues, "Now don't be calling this thing a wheelchair, right! That would be like calling a Shetland pony a mustang. This here thing-a-me is an INDEPENDENCE® iBOT™ 3000 mobility system, a revolutionary device like no other.

"It can balance on two wheels in a complete safety, *stand up* and move around, allowing eye-to-eye contact. If the other person isn't on a horse."

"It will climb up and down stairs with the rider not shifting in the saddle."

"It can travel on dodgy surfaces; grass, gravel, sand, mud, puddles and meadow cakes are all no problem, until you get back to the homestead."

"It also allows you to detach the controls and power the unoccupied device. Like whistling a dog."

"Do I sound like a parrot? That's what the guy who conned us into buying it said? Hope the wheels don't fall off today because it cost a packet."

As Buck goes through his explanation and allows me to play around, I start to understand just how fancy the thing is. I can almost dance. It takes me a few goes to get the hang of each function. Letting it jump up to eye height and balance on two wheels takes quite some getting used to, how we don't fall down in a heap I'll never understand. However, Buck assures me it's safe. He tells me it's all done with mirrors and a piece of string.

Anyway, it all works and has me feeling like a million dollars. I can feel my ear-to-ear grin pull on muscles I haven't used in a while. I try to give Gus a ride, but he jumps down as soon as we move.

It was time to try it out on the stairs so I point myself at the homestead and as a precaution ask Soc if Mother knows anything about the wheelchair. He says, "Holy crap no. Don't be telling her I had anything to do with this. I'm in it up to my ears already. Blame it on these three young whippersnappers. She can have me sack them if you fall off. Before you go, let me put some dust on your boots so she notices you coming."

He picks up some dirt and rubs it over my boots. Then puts a few artistic creations up my clothes, which includes two obvious grope marks on my breasts and a few dusty smudges on my face. "There, that should get you sent back down here for the rest of the day," Soc offers as I start for the house again. He continues with, "Don't be taking too long up there either, Joe. Mullet has some whiz-bang thingummy he needs some help with down here. You remember this is a cattle ranch. We're not running play school for maturing, over active juveniles."

I get to the house. With a little playing around, remembering how Buck had told me to huff and puff, and up the stairs we go. I say nothing, just cruise into the kitchen and do a circuit of the table. Mother keeps working as I float by. I wasn't expected in there so I wasn't noticed. Mother is like that.

I take myself upstairs to check out my proper bedroom. It was just as I had left it, apart from having had an obviously super spring clean and tidy up. I make my way back downstairs re-enter the kitchen and eventually say, "Mother, may I borrow your cars keys please? I seem to have misplaced mine. I'm just on my way into town to pick up a few pizzas for the boys. Shouldn't be long."

Mother goes white, appearing quite ill as she looks at me.

It was disturbing enough to have me feel somewhat guilty. "It's okay Mother, what's done is done. We all have to move on.

"Hey Mother look, no hands."

I pop the chair up into stand-up mode getting a, "Careful Joanne. You might fall."

"It's okay, Mother it's my new wheelchair. The guys had it down in the barn ready to go.

"Anyway, I can't stop. I have to get back. I just wanted to let you know I'm fine. You needn't worry. The guys are great. They'll take care of me." I say it quickly before making a move for the door.

Mother manages to say, "Joanne you have dirt all over you. Come back so I can clean you up."

I pump up my speed a tad to hasten my exit and quickly reply over my shoulder, "Sorry Mother. Have to get back. Love you."

The boys set off inside the barn as I approach, so I follow them. We all finish up in new territory. An office has been added to one corner of the barn where I am invited by Mullet to park myself at the desk while he shows me how to work the new computer that seems to be staring at me.

Mullet says, "Pay attention, Joe. I had to go to Seattle to learn about this damn thing and if it doesn't work, I know Soc is going to sack me. First of all we have our iris recognition feature, which will enable us to navigate the screen. Then we have our voice recognition feature, to help us to do the command functioning and any input. And, if all else fails we have this here mouth-stick to give it a good poke in the keyboard. That should just about cover everything. Oh, and while you're there, would you erase the chat session I had last night with some lady calling herself *Diamond* from New York. If Soc finds out I've been using the computer to pass myself off as a rich cattleman to try to win ladies' hearts, he'll be sure to sack me."

Mullet never was a big talker. When it comes to instructions, he always says if people read too much they're sure to push doors marked *pull*. Anyway, the computer works a treat. In no time flat, I log onto the chat session and send a message to Mullet's new love in New York telling her how much I miss her. I tell her how I can't wait to visit so we can tie each other up and take turns being painted in honey and peanut butter. This gets a good laugh from the gallery behind me.

Soc eventually feels sorry for the lady and reminds us to stop mucking around on company time. He threatens to sack the lot of us. Tells me to start working on the growth figures for next week's cattle sale. And then start working down the list on the desk titled *bookwork I've been meaning to get around to*. The list is seven pages long.

The afternoon flies. Before long I hear the banter of the guys washing up out the front. Stretch comes in and demands I finish up for the day as the beer is waiting to wash the dust down. I don't need to be told twice, although I'm not really looking forward to my first beer through a straw. This is when Stretch explains how he has decided to be my 'beer wench', lifting and holding the beer for me is part of the service. He also explains he has been to Denver to learn how to massage, tone and stimulate unused muscles plus learn how to help quadriplegics cough to clear their airways and a few other tricks. "Come tomorrow we'll be working you over good, and teaching each other some new skills on that table over there." He points and recommends a good night's kip if I want to keep up. Besides, he explains with his usual grin, Soc will be sure to sack us both if he finds us slacking.

It was with some sense of purpose that I went back to the homestead and handed myself over to Mother's care. Somehow being fed, washed and put to bed didn't seem so unbearable. It was quite a joy to notice Mother placing work clothes out for tomorrow. And listen to her lecture my father about making sure those layabouts at the barn clean her boots and dust her down before Joanne puts one foot in this house.

I was only given a light blanket in bed and my grooming was done efficiently. However I could see that even Mother thinks it a wasted effort to overdo the task.

No sooner is the light turned off, than I shoot off to sleep with my mind buzzing and bouncing around through iBot controls, computer commands and cattle weight gains.

I dream the weirdest dream ever. Jess and I were out riding the canyon paddocks when we come upon a heard of Centaurs. They are being supervised and protected by four magnificent specimens standing on a rise overlooking the heard. As we close in on them, they turn to face me. I can clearly make out their quality mustang lines with the torso and faces of Soc, Buck, Mullet and Stretch.

I wake early next morning and take stock while waiting for Mother to come and prepare me for my day. I have no idea what my dream was about, but I'm quite sure it was a message from myself to remind me I'd been a little selfish of late.

I need to think about how things were and how they might have been, without asking why.

I'm not sure what my expectations for myself are just now. However I feel comfortable. I know I'll soon have goals and will be dreaming up plans for the future. My future. My dreams will probably not be as grand as they once might have been. Nevertheless, they'll be real, and I'll make them work. I owe that much to myself. And I owe much, much more to the people who believe in me.

Growing Pains

MY FAMILY HAD SETTLED well in the *west*. Vietnamese village life was but a lingering memory as if it were the plot of some science-fiction novel we read some time ago. Mother missed the old ways, but Father and my two brothers were busy working, "For the dollar," Father would always say and laugh. I didn't miss my old life either, as school here offered so much more. The opportunities of a quality education allowed me to dream my way through any life or profession I could imagine.

It was difficult being the only Vietnamese family in the district. My father and brothers didn't seem to notice. Mother and I could read those quick sideway-glanced leers that would sometimes adorn a passing face. It was almost impossible to blend in, our home being our only true sanctuary of comfortable normality.

I guess school was a little like any new crowded experience. Initially, I was a new toy to some, while others held back to observe and understand me better before stepping forward to share the being known experience. I was never comfortable with the more aggressive males who believed they controlled the sporting fields while maintaining some hierarchy on desirable female form and reminded everyone where girls slotted into the tot. A number of the other girls seemed to relish the attention of these boys. They actively worked their appearance to gain status while playing to Jake, the un-appointed leader. They placed all their dignity at his feet for what seemed to me no reason.

Mostly I kept to myself. I became the object of cruel *jokes* and jeers, particularly on the way home from school, as I needed to navigate the sidewalk where the jocks would park to hang out around Jake's truck. They would just make some hurtful Asian eye and skin remarks with an occasional comment about my small flat form, and of course my ever-present violin case always attracted their scorn. To cross the road or go a different way only made them worse as they would hunt me down. It was best to submit, bow my head and run the verbal gantlet. Mother complained to the school several times but this only made things worse and much more complex. Eventually I kept the taunting to myself, yet even so Mother always seemed to know. Some of my friends would accompany me home, particularly Jennifer who seemed to understand me better than most. She always knew how to control them, knowing when to speak out and what to say. She somehow knew about rude-boy control as if she had been doing courses in it from an early age.

Summer passed quickly, and on prize-giving night, I played my violin in front of the whole school and local community. I felt quite special as I received their applause and many compliments afterwards. Much interest was shown towards the ao dai I chose to wear. Many of the ladies had never seen a traditional Vietnamese costume, and all were rather taken by the feminine elegance of the outfit.

I had no idea my appearance in the ao dai could be a trigger in Jake's mind to pursue me with a different, more personal intent. I noticed a change to his eyes as his regular leers became more personal. He no longer needed an audience surrounding him. To her credit, Jennifer also noticed. She accompanied me home more often while regularly advising me to be careful and try to avoid being near him.

On the evening of my being raped, I was simply walking home from a music lesson when Jake drove up and set upon me. I still struggle with how he could be so naive as to think that through this act I might learn to love him. The violence aside, it was such a humiliating experience, particularly the hospital visits where it seemed everyone on earth had to look at me and receiving stitches in the most private of places was so embarrassing. My confidence evaporated immediately. My mind became consumed by the most horrific of thoughts.

The court case was a bad experience. I was unable to cope with the horrible explanations and questions. Probably because of this, the judge told Jake he was free to go. While I walked out believing I was guilty of many sins and crimes, and forever soiled.

I became a prisoner of my mind and rarely ventured from my room. Anywhere I needed to go, Mother would drive me and be waiting when it was time to return home. At school, Jennifer never left my side. On rare occasions, I would chance upon a visual encounter with Jake. His eyes would penetrate me with a confident lust that cut me apart and would result in my being an incapable, tearful mess for many days. Jake would now always be alone. It appeared he had lost all charismatic hold over his followers.

Winter, summer and winter came and went, and with the passage of the seasons, I realized Jake had seemingly vanished. Eventually I was able to look at myself in the mirror, and the romantic allure slowly inched back into the frequencies emanating from my violin.

One summer afternoon, Jennifer asked if I would accompany her to see her uncle in the local nursing home, and strangely I said yes. Her uncle was a lovely man. He was old beyond his years by a neurological illness, which made his every movement a mammoth effort. He was very dependent on others for his needs, a *prisoner* in his body and small room. Yet his mind was so active and bright with his face still exhibiting the contours of a thousand fulfilling experiences. To my surprise and delight, he spoke fluent Vietnamese. He was even familiar with the geography around my birth village and was the first person I have met since leaving Vietnam able to pronounce my name correctly. He even knew that my name *Hung* was literally a pink rose. We shared a joke about the commonness of our family names, saying we must be related somehow as his name was *Jones* and mine was *Nguyen*. I felt quite relaxed talking with him. I even realized my Vietnamese fluency was childish and would always remain so unless I actively developed my birth culture further. Jennifer and I walked home together. I was able to hold a smile to my face for the first time in so long.

I think it might have been my fifth visit to Jennifer's uncle. It was the time Jennifer persuaded me to wear an ao dai, and seeing her uncle's face made the experience worthwhile. Visiting Jennifer's uncle was always a rich and joyful experience for us all. It was while we were leaving that we noticed a young man in a wheelchair approaching the door from the other side. We opened the door and gave him space. I could not help noticing what a mess this poor man was. A strap around his chest supported his torso from falling forward, and his worthless legs dangled onto a support attached to his compact wheelchair. His right hand had all the fingers missing, leaving the obvious mark of a single blow from something like a meat-clever. His face carried the permanent scars of many blows and slashes. As he struggled towards us, I noticed his head drop with that look people use when they want to disappear. Only then did I notice it was

Jake. He courageously motioned a humbled *thank you* for holding the door. This gesture enabled me to notice his tongue had also been severed.

Jennifer and I walked to her car speechless. Eventually I asked did she know what had happened to him. Jennifer told me she knew he had been assaulted but had no idea how permanent his injuries were. That night I did some soul-searching. I tried to feel sorry for Jake but I had no tears left. Strangely, I felt quite comfortable and secure. I slept all night undisturbed waking more relaxed then I'd done in many years.

A Passing Moment

IT WAS WITH SOME CONVICTION I entered the bathroom looking for a vacant cubical. The orange juice after lunch had seemed a good idea at the time.

It wasn't until I was washing my hands, I noticed her. She was on the floor, back against the wall. Slender arms embracing shapely legs, which were squeezed against her chest. She was looking up towards me. On her knee was a red mark where her chin had recently rested. Her eyes were dry though puffy rings around them exposed their recent history.

I asked if she was okay, and while I didn't hear a sound in reply, her pretty face lit up spelling comfort as her lips and eyes motioned a message leaving me with no reason to worry for her.

I returned her smile and quickly hurried for class as it was English and *Baroness Black Skirt* already had me on report for being late this week.

The last ten minutes of our lesson in dominant self-indulged ranting seemed like an hour thirty. I was sitting cross-legged with a somewhat urgent desire to retrace my steps to the bathroom. The clock seemed to travel painfully slow.

Finally free, I rushed to the bathroom. She was still there. I'm not sure why, but I sat beside her and without saying a word took her soft, warm hand in mine to ask what the problem was.

We exchanged names before she told me today was to be her last day at school. Tomorrow she was to travel to Iran where it had been arranged for her to marry a cousin. All her western talk of a university education, refusing to wear traditional headdress and speaking out of place had pushed her family too far.

Eventually I excused myself to use the bathroom. When I returned she was no longer there. I ran outside and searched for her. She was gone.

Everywhere I go now I look for SoulmAz. Any success, achievement or liberties comes with need, a burning conscious desire to share.

A Further Moment

I GUESS IT TOOK SIX weeks at university to decide teaching was a career best suited for someone else. Yet I finished my degree and numbly taught English for three years before addressing the obvious.

One morning while screeching at a student, who dared to yawn in my class, I witnessed a haunting expression of hurt and perplexed loathing. In that instant I realized I had become what I dreaded most in my youth, the reincarnation of a teacher I'd labelled *Baroness Black Skirt*. The notion of another generation of adolescent dreams cruelly stolen and crushed was too much. I found my way to explore the uncertainty of the employment-classified jungle that very day.

For some time I lingered, introduced myself to the kitchen of fast-food outlets, a car wash and the view from a high-rise window-cleaning platform. I even tried a receptionist job at a gymnasium with links to the underworld. The experiences were all more satisfying then teaching, but my pocket yearned for stability and the on-flowing rewards. Eventually I wandered into print journalism, writing social columns for the tribune. Our circulations are good and on the up. My non-de-plume and ultra ego *Caprice Savoy* is a hit with the readers. Cynical assessment of the social set at work and play makes quite a splash on the street. Although, in the polite circles of local society the term *gutter* press is bantered about regularly for many of the more revealing exposures.

For myself, I write the entertainment pages under my own name, Jennifer Priestly. Nothing flash, just a few book reviews, what's hot at the movies, the odd live show and upcoming local events. My editor keeps it so to conceal Caprice Savoy's true identity. It leaves me free to ply my real trade writing cutting social articles free from direct scrutiny and pressure that powerful people can't resist applying.

Those in the know have labelled me with the charming office nickname of *Butt Boy*. It's rather clever. Insiders use it openly to thank me in front of everyone by acknowledging I'd crawl through garbage to get a juicy take on someone who deserves negative publicity to match their behaviour. While on the office floor they believe it's an unflattering sexist label reserved for a fairly useless, mature yet junior single female. Someone thrown scraps of stories between assignments of carrying tea and coffee for the bosses; sexism is not altogether rare in the corridors of journalism. But not to worry, all this gets me through doors. Allows me to watch and hear the bitchy gossip without the slightest suspicions coming my way. I'm quite sure many of the often outraged feel sorry for me while wishing festering spots for the allusive Caprice Savoy and his sexist editor.

On the private front, my life is a total mess and without hope. I live alone in a bed-sit, save for half-eaten take-away and multiple almost-empty alcohol bottles that rotate regularly. Scotch straight from the bottle is my drug of choice.

Even my cat chose to move next door and live with the two gay guys. They care for him much better than I do. If it comes down to it, they care for me better than I do. They sit me at their table surrounded by fresh vegetables with all the trimmings every once in a while. I suspect it may be just supervised visitation access to my cat. Perhaps they do it to get me out of lounging around drinking in nothing but underwear every weekend. Either way, I appreciate their support. The three of them, the gay guys and my cat, are the only people in the world I look forward to meeting and can truly label as friends.

I've been through several relationships and one husband to descend this far down with my life. All ended in tears and broke my heart almost beyond recovery. In my late twenties I even tried a *special* girlfriend. We were together for some time. That too ended in tears, her tears. It broke my heart when I realized how completely I'd broken hers.

%%%%

The note on my desk from the editor said, and I quote, "Butt boy, get you arse out to see what this is all about." It was scribbled across a press release for an author promoting her new book titled, *The Myths Behind the Veil*. The fourth novel by some author I'd never heard of, SoulmAz Khanum.

The press release said, *The Myths Behind the Veil* is a best seller in France and is sweeping the western world.

Ms Khanum's résumé is rather impressive:

Bachelor of Arts and Entertainment from the university of Tehran

Bachelor of Media Studies from Bu-Ali Sina university

Master of Media Studies Sorbonne university

Doctor of Philosophy with a major in modern literature university of Bonn

Fluent in seven languages and currently Reader of Literature at the Sorbonne faculty of literature studies.

As if this wasn't enough to make me sick, she's been married for twenty-two years, has two teenage children, a boy and a girl -—of course -—and her husband is a principle violinist with the orchestra of Paris. And, if her photo is a real likeness, she's drop-dead gorgeous; not one of your half-starved catwalk-strutting, clothing–rack-gorgeous. Her smile is warm and confident, elegance oozing and it sits on top of a tall slim, curvy feminine shaped structure. A package to turn heads and linger long after the door closes behind her behind.

The flier explains how SoulmAz lives permanently in France, as living in Iran offends her husband, who is also an Iranian native but will not live anywhere that doesn't afford his partner and daughter the right to hold a driver's licence or pursue any activity their heart might desire.

The press release also explains how SoulmAz likes to unwind and collect her thoughts driving a BMW Z4 Roadster through the French countryside with the top down. The car, the fourth love in her life, was a gift from her family for her thirty-fifth birthday.

I scorn and think unflattering thoughts while making an appointment to interview a *cash-cow*. My day is finished off deep in thought with my Caprice hat on. A juicy little page three titbit, titled *When is enough never enough,* revealing a bored socialite wife with a secret lust for both the gardener and the neighbour's teenage son. A story of a protagonist deserving of all the attention our media can provide.

On the way home I drop into a bookstore and purchase a copy of *The Myths Behind the Veil* to help prepare for tomorrow's interview.

I walk into my flat and wade through pizza boxes. I make my way towards the kitchen table intending to clear a space to unload my shackles. Something is wrong. All the takeaway wrappers and bottles are on the floor. I was sure some should be on the table; it's the law of averages. Wait, the table has a book on it, titled *The Myths Behind the Veil.* A Post-It note is inviting attention. A stylish confident hand has written, *page forty-seven; r*ead.

The scene is a school washroom with two girls sitting on the floor. One is trying to help the other survive the onset of an uncertain future. I skip the second-hand-food I'd planned for dinner and read most of the night. Even forgetting my walk-on role, this novel is a bestseller. "What a writer! Oh wow, SoulmAz what have you done? All these years I've been searching, reaching and worrying about you for no reason."

On the last page there is another Post-it note in the same confident handwriting. It reads, *Jennifer, I'm so glad I've finally found you. Don't be alarmed by the seemingly ineffective locks. The charming guys next door let me in. Sorry I missed you; until tomorrow, your loving friend, SoulmAz. (A big kiss.)——PS: Jennifer. We need to talk. You're living like an Iranian goat herder!*

Wiping back tears, I read the last page.

Before finding my bed for the night I drain all the non-empty bottles of whiskey down the sink and make a good start on cleaning my flat.

A Precious Moment

WE SPENT A DAY AND a half employing people to work on my appearance. The finished product; fair to average, probably six or seven on a scale of ten. The result; my skin felt too soft to touch without bruising and the false nails were driving me crazy, although my paint looked quite dapper and the patterns were growing on me. I found myself removing my shoes every other hour just to wiggle my toes re-checking the artwork. They were kind-of cute, a first for me. I'm not a foot person and I don't do cute.

Most of the people involved in the transformation were ultra polite and almost able to hide the expression they reserve for first visits of a reformed, off the shelf, K-Mart shopper. It was rather obvious how the old 'battle-axe' boutique owner, who tried to flog us all the evening wear, dropped the word 'elegant' from her well rehearsed third person *'madam'* something praise line, the moment she watched me try to move in heels. I assume her charming young assistant will manage to keep her job if she looks remorseful and doesn't openly giggle again throughout the customer etiquette reinforcement lecture she will no doubt receive.

Eventually we all resolved to settle for a number of better-cut business suits with heelless shoes suitable for students at an upmarket ladies-college. It's just as well my feet are smallish and I'm six foot one tall, they all said in some polite form. Still, I could see from their faces they thought I must have been raised in a one-room cabin high in the mountains somewhere to have never acquired any skill in the gentle art of walking on heels.

It was embarrassing walking into work looking like, *Barbie's aunty Gladys,* as some loud 'pig' from the sports desk piped out. There were a few wolf whistles, two back slaps, which I truly hate, and one kind-of proposal of marriage with a rather rude tongue gesture thrown in. The editor even slipped from his office and remarked loud enough for everyone to hear, "It's amazing what a coat of varnish will do to an old yawl. Butt Boy, as soon as you dump those parcels, my office. Feel free to bring a coffee for yourself if you can manage it without spilling mine."

I was seated in the editor's office sipping coffee before he confessed there was nothing to talk about, business wise. It seems he just likes the way I make coffee and wanted to tell me again how proud he was to have someone from the *Tribune* actually invited to lunch at the national press club, in Washington DC. It didn't matter to him the speaker was my good friend and author, *SoulmAz Khanum*. He had *'Our Man in Washington'* written across the front page of his minds eyes.

I slipped my shoes off and showed him my toes with a wiggle saying, "What about these for a guy-magnet." We shared a laugh agreeing they looked dangerous. I even noticed he dropped his guard for an instant, as if drifting back in time alone. He must have been quite some spunk before family, editorial responsibility, and grey hair consumed him.

The editor sent me home to take my time packing for the flight. He told me to go pick up my stuff and rush off as if on an urgent assignment and stood at his office door making bold statements about, *it had better be front page or you can keep going*, just to reinforce his office image.

The flight was a good one, which suited me because I'm not at all confident about what keeps aircraft from falling. The taxi ride Reagan airport to the Henley Park hotel was by comparison much more hair-raising, what with my driver's compulsive need to speed, change lanes on a whim, use back alleys and delight in pointing out intricate detail of recent drive-by shootings, mugging, murders and rapes without displaying any need to hold the steering wheel or look through the windscreen for more than an occasional glance.

The hotel was delightful, just as well as I settled in for the night, too afraid to accompany a head full of muggings and murders on an evening stroll around town. I dined and slept well, waking freshly relaxed ready for my day in the national capital.

By design, the hotel was only a few blocks along Massachusetts Avenue from the national press club. I decided to leg it, leaving early enough to find my way but not so early as to arrive looking like someone's country cousin doing the once in a lifetime Washington thing.

It's funny how we occasionally chance upon people with an undefined something that draws our eyes to follow them uncontrollably, while we sub-consciously busy our brain compiling a wish list about whom or what they might be. He even looked familiar. Dressed in a business suit, not a particularly expensive cut though his body filled it suitably. Lustful staring seemed acceptable to a point. I'm not sure where he came from, as I approached the press club he walked into view from the side crossing my path and entered the building a little in front of me. There was confidence in his walk. He obviously knew where he was going. I quickly had him down as a Washington Post journalist at least, married, a few kids, a multi-million dollar house, his and her sports cars plus an SUV for shopping.

My familiar stranger went straight for the dining hall and furthered my curiosity by speaking briefly at the reception desk before being ushered around the security people without the necessity of passing through the metal detector. *Wow,* I thought, before being distracted asking where I needed to go at the front desk. I was sent in his footsteps to reception at the dinning hall. No such service for me; there were lists to look though with some cross checking, a visitor name tag to be found and secured to my person, which was then removed along with everything metallic in preparation for running the electronic gauntlet.

The stylish blouse with the genuine gold thread through it had seemed like a wonderful fashion statement until it got me rejected three times by the metal detector and rapidly brought several well dressed, suitably alarmed bouncers my way. I was done over twice with a hand wand before being ushered aside in the direction of a portable cubical, where I discovered, private and very comprehensive frisking is undertaken. Even my choice in under-wire bra couldn't be visually explained, needing to be removed to get me through a beep-less wave of the wand. Standing under arrest for several minutes, while someone was found with attire resembled a female, in full view of amused press people keen to manufacture a story, kept me thinking what a poor job I was doing at maintaining a low profile. When the press photographers started taking my photo surrounded by security guards, I couldn't help feeling a flashing light on my head saying, *out-of-town hick,* would have done the same job with much less drama.

I finally got myself certified beep free, and re-dressed to be presentable enough to find my way into the dining room proper. Sure, I was ruffled around the edges but my having not gone ahead fitting an IUD last year somehow made me feel better. As it happens, I was just in time to witness my mystery man helping himself to a table upgrade. He switched name-place holders from the back corner to the centre, not far from the speaker. His behaviour didn't offend me, I've done the same many times; journalism is not a profession for the meek. My natural curiosity took me straight to the centre table to read the name-place label. Two things struck me, firstly his name, *'Jason Slaughter'* and second he was now seated next to me. I thought, *wow lucky break*, before the penny dropped, *no wonder he looked familiar.* I spent a whole summer in my school days, learning about heartbreak, necking with a Jason Slaughter. In those days I was too young and innocent to do anything memorable, other than hold hands in public and rub anything above the waist for hours when alone. Nothing ever came of our encounters. I grew up while he still had zits. And besides, he took up football; it was impossible to get near him the way the cheer squad groupies were. He had made an impact on me though, for some time I was sure of being doomed to hell for allowing him to use his tongue while kissing and I got grounded big-time when a neighbour told my mother I was allowing boys to venture inside my blouse. The last I heard Jason Slaughter he'd joined the marines. I guess he was the last person I expected to see wearing a suit in a club for journalists.

I decided to play it cool. By the time he sat beside me and did the, "Jennifer Priestly, well I never... how are you! I'm Jason Slaughter. We went to school together."

I looked at him and said, "Jason Slaughter. The name sounds familiar but in all honesty I can't place you. I'll check through my schoolbook tonight. Do you have a card?"

I opened my purse and passed him my card in a well-rehearsed gesture. In truth I was fishing for more information about him. He didn't offer his card.

He just looked at mine and said, "I'm confused. This card belongs to Caprice Savoy. Are you moonlighting?"

I almost looked at the card, but pulled myself up in time. It seems our man who doesn't like going through metal detectors is very, very well informed. The waitress placing a meal in front of me saved me to some extent. The exchange wasn't over. This guy was rapidly becoming my number one priority for investigative journalism. Nothing ticks me off more than people who use privileged information to re-enforce a position of power over others. Especially me.

The meal was a delight; I went for the Chicken Kiev with a Chocolate Soufflé dessert. The wine list was most impressive. I stuck to mineral water, in keeping with my recently created self-image. The other guests at the table bantered small talk back and forward. They clearly knew each other well and I knew several by site. All seemed to want to know more about me. Basically they were fishing to find out how I managed to score a seat at the prestigious centre table.

When the manager introduced SoulmAz to the table. I earned status, having SoulmAz refer to me by name and embrace me warmly without an introduction. My table companions were particularly impressed when SoulmAz arranged for me to meet tonight in her Hotel. Business Cards were rapidly exchanged with me, from all. Jason was quickly dropped from the conversation. Everyone present knew he belonged in the back corner. Besides a guy without a business card in these circles must be an impostor or a joke.

I was delightfully surprised to establish just how esteemed SoulmAz was. During her speech all hung to her every word. Consumed by the logic she presented in her arguments, seduced with the skill of how her words captured attention. She spoke of the right of children to grow up healthy and free from oppression. She spoke of her dream that women will one day be masters of their own destiny, equal partners in the business of owning and determining worldly needs. Afterwards she fielded questions and in every case was able to offer answers... solutions to delight an enlightened audience. She received a standing ovation for her effort, quite an achievement in a room overflowing with journalistic cynicism. The conversation at our table continued for some time after SoulmAz had left for her next engagement. Not the journalism face of a situation, but an exchange of ideas offered and received by equals who had found a desire to expand their knowledge base and gain a better understanding of the people around them.

I walked out of the press club freshly enlightened with six new valuable journalist contacts and Jason on my arm. He offered to show me the sights of Washington during what remained of the afternoon. I'm sure it was no accident Jason found the time to show me round. I faked a trip to the bathroom to phone my editor and establish his take on Jason. I was quickly cautioned I was probably dealing with a genuine CIA operative investigating what threat factors may be associated with, and around, SoulmAz. I thought this sounded silly but if I might quote my editor, *'be careful with those guys. They are all dangerously crazy. They hear and see threats to national security in every Pizza order. The environment they work in goes to their head.'*

I quickly took up Jason's offer to show me his town but my editor's words were starting to affect me. I even wondered if he was the Jason Slaughter of my youth. Perhaps he was a stranger, pretending. I searched his demeanour for something, a sign to reassure me and could find nothing convincingly familiar.

First on the national capital scenic tour was, *'The Wall.'* He took me straight to his brother's name, running his hand over the lettering like an alcoholic might fondle the last empty gin bottle. He talked of duty, what it means to be a true patriot.

I was starting to catch on to his wavelength but said nothing. I sat back for the ride as we drove across the Potomac to Arlington Cemetery, which he could only refer to as Fort Myer. We went straight for Kennedy's grave, where he seemed to say a quiet prayer. I used the opportunity to take out my camera and started photographing things so as to include Jason. I asked about the impressive backdrop, Arlington House, and was fascinated to discover this 'knowledgeable' patriot had no idea he was standing in the historical grounds of the Lee family residence. That this magnificent tribute to national pride and human sacrifice was created out of political vindictiveness had been skipped from the training he received. The quote, *'Those who don't study history are condemned to relive it,'* rolled in and out of my brain, though I knew better than to share it.

I guessed correctly. Next stop was the Iwo Jima memorial. And again, I received a meaning of patriotism talk. Two charming Japanese tourists interrupted us, asking if I would take a photo of them together, in front of the monument. They were such a beautiful happy couple, obviously very much in love and mesmerizing in front of a camera. I asked permission to take their photo using my own camera, warning them I was a newspaper journalist writing an article about visiting Washington. We exchanged bows and business cards. To them it would be a family honour appearing in print. I asked the man if he would take a photo of Jason and myself, putting my arm under Jason's shoulder in a best buddies pose and changed sides to repeat the embrace for another photo.

Jason was, shall we say, a little put out that Japanese people would dare visit 'his' sacred memorial.

I wasn't sympathetic. My conversation with the young couple had revealed, between them, they had lost three great uncles to the fighting on Iwo Jima Island. I realised how this monument commemorated our combined history. Bringing our nations closer together. This memorial was as much for them as it was mine.

Jason's attitudes and obsessions were really started to bug me. I only arranged the photo shoot to check for a shoulder holster, which was surely there, under his left arm.

Time was running low. I asked to be taken to the hotel to prepare for my appointment with SoulmAz. In the privacy of his car Jason opened up. It seems I was in danger and needed protection. SoulmAz represented a threat to national security. It was his duty to watch her and make sure I didn't become involved. According to Jason, I would be well advised to stand her up tonight and not have anything to do with her in the future. I laughed openly in his face; it didn't go over well. He was most definitely the Jason of my past. I once rather foolishly told him he was acting out a gay fantasy spending so much time interacting in the change room with his football buddies. I saw the same threatening expression then; he had not changed one bit over the years. He didn't speak, choosing to sit quietly stewing. Glancing at me occasionally; it was as if he retracted into a sulking provoked rage. I remember at school it made me feel concerned for my safety. He looked so dangerously untrustworthy. It was the reason I broke off with him. Nothing had changed, all the feelings and emotions came flooding back, save that I'm now street toughened. I found another quote floating around inside my head and said it out loud, *'Patriotism is the last refuge of a scoundrel,'* Though I'm not sure why. I was quite sure my nationalistically indoctrinated travelling companion wouldn't have the foggiest understanding what it meant.

The journalist in me took over. Started me asking questions, using my most seductive presentation to have him explain his idiom further. The guy was crazy. To him, being from Iran and having a funny name was the threat. Oh, and being successful enough to draw a crowd was clearly very dangerous. He didn't say so but I'm sure being female, as well, made SoulmAz deadly dangerous. I asked about his research to date, had he read her books and while he skirted the questions he finally admitted being a patriot meant having a responsibility to set an example and not read subversive trash. I asked further about the research he had undertaken to reach the conclusion SoulmAz was such a threat and followed his silence with a battery of questions about her past; where she grow up, where she now lives, her work, family, friends etc. Jason skipped around and grew quite uncomfortable. Starting to talk down, at me, playing the need to know, secrets game, enough to convince me he knew nothing at all about SoulmAz, good or bad.

Jason followed me to my room where I invited him to pour a drink from the mini-bar while I deliberately changed in front of him. There was no real reason to change but I wanted to expose Jason's psyche. What better way to unravel him than place some flesh in his face, all very innocent of course. I wanted to watch him exercise some of his ideological restraint. After all, I'm mixing in dangerous circles. He needs to avoid subversive trash. I maintained a conversation and proceeded to strip without covering up or even turning away, as if I do this all the time. He sipped, talked and watched. Somewhere during the display he ran out of words, made up for the silence with additional watching. Never one to miss an opportunity I went to the bathroom leaving the door open, having already made sure he was seated where we would maintain eye contact. I used the washbasin to give myself a sponge down, the like of which I hadn't experienced since bumming around Europe many years ago.

I changed the topic to the immoral influence of rock music while I did my hair and applied some make-up. All the while maintaining nakedness like it was completely natural. I guessed correctly, to Jason rock musicians was a threat. This was my cue to talk about Jeff Baxter and his involvement with the missile defence agency. I enjoyed explaining how he was known as Skunk when playing guitar in Steely Dan and the Doobie Brothers. I'm quite sure Jason didn't know I was trying to wind him up further. Everything seemed to pass over the head of a brain occupied by nakedness on parade. His eyes followed my every move while exhibiting lustful need. The fill of his trousers was sending signals of masculine approval.

Satisfied I had his full attention I commenced to dress. Did the job slowly, asking his advice about which piece to wear and help with bra clasps, etc. To his credit he kept his hands to himself and made no advances other than numerous complements designed to draw the conversation towards sexual matters to focus on getting physical. It didn't work. I kept right on talking. Anything to do with matters of national security, policy or patriotic duty, for no reason other than to tease his masculinity into submission.

I invited Jason to be my guest for the evening. He accepted in an instant. The principles involved with visiting SoulmAz and her family had seemed to become irrelevant. Jason wanted to follow me anywhere after what I'd just put him through. He was feeling lucky about his chances tonight.

The evening with SoulmAz was a delight. Her husband and children were as enlightened, charming and confident, as I knew they would be. I introduced Jason as an old friend who had also attended the same school, adding; he is a genuine, gun packing CIA spy these days. I also explained, for Jason's benefit, how our parents all still lived within a few blocks of each other.

Everyone received a surprise with my introduction of Jason. SoulmAz's son instantly became Jason's biggest fan and wanted to talk spy things all night. I used the opportunity to take their photo together with Jason proudly displaying his CIA identity pass on his chest. Jason was speechless, simply floored and somewhat embarrassed to discover the connection between SoulmAz and myself, and also himself.

It was rather late when we reached my hotel. Jason had a look of expectation in his eyes. I invited him in, poured drinks and sat close, offering the latitude to accept advances. His hands were soft and gentle, graceful. I wasn't expecting this to be so. I had prepared myself for a torrid time, mindful of teenagers experimenting. How heavy handed he was with my chest. Although in those days I knew no better either.

His hands confidently found their way to my shoulders, travelled under my hair, slowly drawing me forward, our lips met half way. First a few innocent pecks before increasing in intensity and the embrace. Soft caresses drove me further into the motion of his spell. Hands manoeuvred behind and below my ears where fingers found unmarked places to heighten the sensation of my involvement. The cool dampness of his motioning lips sent signals to search for buttons on his shirt. Each in turn gave over their capture of him allowing my fingers to navigate, blindly feeling across masculine contours, venturing further.

The pulsating of my heart pumping consciousness into an expanding chest of heightened sensation, magical tingles engulfed me as Jason released the inhibitions of my clothing. His hands ventured lower, occasionally softly rising to sweep up and outwards engulfing the form of my tightening breasts. Caressed with a touch of tongue supported between lips of gold.

We stood continuing to undress, not breaking the emotional embrace holding us. We stared for a microsecond our naked venerability alone with each other, identical, displaying and surveying the differences drawing us together. On the bed we accepted each other as one. Our motion gyrated in cooperative unison, electric, wanting to move faster, stay perfectly still, throwing us deeper into the moment of being one. The lustful bliss of orgasm visited me several times. We rolled taking control of each other until in an explosive release of energy we climaxed together before subsiding into quiet motionlessness.

In the dim light of the room I watched him lay like a contented baby, my head resting on his shoulder. I watched him fall asleep and wondered of what he would dream. I thought at length of him as a raw teenager and pondered where he gained his experience. Somewhere in my thoughts the events of the day closed in, racing consciousness gave way to sleep.

We woke still tangled in our embrace, the room captured by daylight holding messages of sunshine etched on closed curtains. There was time for a relaxing breakfast, in bed, followed by a clean up, together, in a bath full of bubbles before it was time for me to return home. I've always been partial to a good back scrub and neck massage from kind hands, so I left the room feeling at my best. We allowed ourselves some folly, taking Jason's photo, my action man, dressed only in his shoulder holster draped across my bed, in waiting.

Jason drove me to the airport, said a passionate farewell; very impressive. I guess he had fallen in deeper than I thought possible. On the plane I started mapping out two articles. One by Jennifer Priestly titled *'The Diversity of our National Capital,'* the centrepiece being the beautiful image of the Japanese couple standing in front of the Iwo Jima memorial, a sure grab to capture reader attention. The article was the usual, where to go, what to see society pages rubbish, plus a summary of SoulmAz's speech and vision.

The other Article was by Caprice Savoy titled, *'Our Man in Washington – on the Job.'* I had our imaging department make a composite to clean up Jason dressed only in his shoulder holster. They enlarged and positioned his CIA identity pass over him, made him decent, suitable for publication, but stole nothing from the image in terms of reader imagination. The story detail was a believable nameless fabrication, presenting an argument about paranoid CIA agents, out of control, accountable to no one, inventing enemies, using power and position to manipulate people for personal gratification.

They say a picture is worth a thousand words, my editor beamed with delight while signing off on the story, he shook his head mumbling, "Butt Boy you evil, evil person. This is so precious. I love you. The punters do so like a good, well told conspiracy theory."

We received a lot of feedback about the articles. Both caught our readers' imaginations. The editor received the usual gutter press complaints about Caprice Savoy, and numerous requests to purchase the article for re-print in other newspapers, some from the national press; an excellent day in editor circles.

Eventually the call I was expecting came through. It was in the form of a text message from Jason saying simply, *'You heartless bitch.'* An uncomfortable smirk came to my face. I had obviously made an impression. That's what good journalism is about; I told myself.

Without saying a word I retrieved some text I keyed in earlier. My reply was a quote, *'Truth is the first casualty of war.'* It seemed the right thing to say. Jason and I were never meant to be.

Warrior Chick

IT WAS ONLY EIGHT IN the morning yet the mercury was nudging one hundred degrees on the sun-soaked Parvan soil of eastern Afghanistan. Lieutenant Kelly Cassidy sat in a cockpit at the controls of her aircraft, which was neatly parked in the keyhole entrance slightly off the end of the ten thousand foot runway at Bagram Airfield. It was Kelly's turn to play *the waiting game,* a polite colloquial term given to rapid deployment stand-by duties. Her Fairchild Republic Thunderbolt II, A10 warthog, was loaded to the teeth with an array of weaponry, fuelled to capacity, ready for action, and waiting.

Kelly had just commenced her third hour of boredom and was starting to become aware of stiffness in her rear end. Were it not for the luxury of a beach umbrella erected above her head and a tattered romance novel she was reading for the seventh time, she would almost certainly have dozed off into her favourite hallucination involving dust-free, bluegrass fields near Paris, Kentucky and a hot tub full to the rim with beautiful bubbles and sweet-smelling perfumes.

On the ground beside the aircraft fuselage in the shade of the wing lay master sergeant Josie Alderman, her green tee shirt tied to help simulate sun-baking on a Florida beach. Josie was reading one of the two Man magazines she'd traded with a grunt the night before, for six small chocolate bars and twenty-three cigarettes. Josie was a little embarrassed to be reading a Man magazine but she was desperate for something new in her life, and she told herself she was reading the magazine for the articles not the pictures, but she kept turning the magazine sideways every now and then, like the guys who say the same thing do.

Both ladies lifted their heads as the unmistakable sound of a C141B Startlifter lumbered along the taxiway towards them. It was the 8am *ticket home.* Every morning one of these monsters climbed into the sky and disappeared in the direction of Germany en route to the states. Everyone at Bagram stopped to watch it take off. Kelly and Josie stared at the plane as it approached, turned in front of them, roared and commenced to disappear away from them towards home. The moment the main wheels left the ground, both ladies mumbled, "lucky people." Their gaze remained fixed on the plane as it slowly shrank into the dusty grey-blue Afghan sky.

No sooner had each lady returned to the pages of her book when the plane's radio shattered the calm, "Warthog EL207 this is Bagram tower. Your services have been requested by airborne command prepare for takeoff and await further instruction."

Kelly immediately pressed her radio response button saying, "This is warthog EL207 will comply, out."

By the time Kelly finished speaking, Josie had jumped to her feet, climbed the access ladder, folded and thrown the beach umbrella and the novel onto the tarmac a considerable distance behind her. She was leaning into the cockpit removing a series of red tagged pins attached to the safety harness, designed to render much of the aircraft's numerous switches and controls, unusable while stationary on the ground. As each pin was removed, Josie held it up for an instant, allowing Kelly's eyes to acknowledge it before the pin was placed into the small locker beside and behind Kelly's head. Meanwhile Kelly was busy talking to herself while working a series of switches and paddling at flight controls. Dials and gauges were lighting-up while various parts of the aircraft commenced to rattle, buzz, whirl or click. With an expanding whistle, the engines commenced to breathe as they rapidly journeyed towards life, a rumble, some shaking, a roar and the squeak of brakes completed the metamorphism of silent metal into a living breathing *war bird.*

Josie removed the last of the pins from the ACES II ejection seat and stowed it in the locker. She raised her thumb, saying, "Go get them, Killer. And look after my aircraft."

Kelly acknowledged with a raised thumb and a twinkle from her left eye. By the time Kelly returned to her controls, Josie was on the ground, had stowed the access ladder, closed the ladder locker and was running around the aircraft removing more red tags, small covers and the wheel chocks. In no more than ten seconds, Josie stood forward of the left wing tip her thumb raised above her head, watching.

Kelly again raised her thumb. The aircraft immediately rolled forward, parts of the wing began to grow and the canopy commenced to close. Without moving her lips, Josie uttered, "Please! Come back safely, Ma'am."

Kelly spoke into the radio, "Bagram control this is warthog EL207. We are ready and standing by. Awaiting your instruction."

The radio responded, "EL207, you are clear for take-off on runway three seven, barrier down. Climb to ten thousand feet and await instruction from airborne command. Good hunting."

Kelly turned onto the runway, locked the nose wheel and moved the condition levers fully forward. The two General Electric TF34 turbofans screamed and rumbled while seven thousand two hundred horsepower focused on pushing Kelly forward at a rapidly increasing speed. Kelly spoke into the radio, "Rolling", followed a short time later by, "Committed."

JOSIE STARED AT KELLY as they were consumed by distance. After what seemed like ages, Kelly raised the nose and started skyward. As the wheels retracted, Josie blew a kiss and called out loudly, "Godspeed, ma'am. Come back safely; love you."

KELLY THROTTLED BACK to seventy-five percent as she climbed through seven thousand feet and steadied her rate of climb to save fuel. As she reached nine thousand feet the radio emitted, "Warthog EL207 this is Widow Maker on-board sentry. Please respond."

A smile entered Kelly's heart to hear the voice and unmistakable call sign of Wendy Maiden, her roommate at officer school, the class of ninety-six. Kelly spoke to the radio, "Widow Maker this is Killer Chick flying EL207 at your service. What can we do for you this morning?"

Wendy's voice responded, "Hey there Killer. How are they hanging? We have a situation to the east requiring your expertise. You will be in a loitering role. We have a group of our gents delayed at their pick-up zone by an unserviceable chinook. Your presence has been requested in a precautionary capacity as they exposed their position prior to the chopper delay. I am arming your displays now.

You will notice your journey and destination proximity to the Pakistan border. We urge you to take all precaution in this regard."

Kelly again spoke into her radio, "Will comply. Nice to hear you are still sleeping with clean sheets, Widow. I'll be in touch as I approach the destination, in seventy minutes. Killer, out."

The radio spoke up again, "Negative Killer, we require you on site in fifty minutes. Don't worry about the fuel tab, we will take care of it. We have our extender here, and it will be at your disposal. Widow, over."

"Will comply. Fifty minutes it is. Killer out."

Kelly immediately throttled up to ninety percent and while continuing her climb, she banked right to align herself on a bearing of thirty-eight degrees, matching the navigational heading indicator now showing on her head-up display.

Kelly climbed to eighteen thousand feet before levelling out. Her route would weave a little to avoid overflying populated areas, as was the custom. She flew to the northeast, tracking between Karak and Esl Shafi, to the north of Atiti and Welo, the south of Shahran where she commences to track further northeast, into Badakhshan State skirting the border of Pakistan's North-West Frontier province. The rugged Hindu Kush mountains *climbed* higher in front of the plane. The ridges and peaks were now capped with snow and only a few thousand feet below. After passing Deh Gol, Kelly headed further eastward, along the Wakhan corridor where she could clearly see Turkistan to the north as well as Pakistan to the south. She passed south of Kand Khan and again headed further eastward to track south of Deh Gholaman, where she allowed her thoughts to drift for a second, wondering if Marco Polo thought this place looked like hell when he passed through here all those years before. *At least I don't have to walk, and I will not be taking four years.*

Kelly was now cutting straight across the high ridges and steep sided valleys, giving quite a sensation of speed as the land kept dropping away suddenly, only to rapidly rise up again in what seemed like only a few yards. The country below was the usual hot or freezing, dusty, rugged brown offering, totally devoid of vegetation save for an attempt at a green strip in the valley floor near the winding stream that always occupied these valleys. Kelly shook her head, contemplating why anyone would choose to live here and used the remaining flight minutes to carry out diagnostics on her weapons and flight systems. Everything appeared to be working fine, a rarity. *Must be my lucky day,* she thought.

WITH HER POSITION DUE south of Sarhadd, Kelly banked sharply right to travel south following a narrow, steep valley that headed to Barrogil in Pakistan. She could see the road below winding along the western wall of the inhospitable valley.

Kelly throttled back to only thirty percent and adjusted her controls to keep the nose from rising. This allowed a considerable reduction in speed and the commencement of a rather rapid descent while appearing to be in level flight. She was about to speak into the radio when it came to life, like magic. "Killer this is Widow. You have made good time. Your hosts are thirty-five miles in front of you and will be four degrees left of your current heading. They are in a defensive position on a small outcrop just above the valley floor at seven thousand eight hundred feet. Their friendly status should be appearing on your displays. I'm patching you into direct contact with Greenhead on channel eighty-seven. You are to maintain a listening watch on this channel at all times. You should take precautions for the possibility of surface to air missile attack at low altitudes in this area, out."

Kelly acknowledged the message, set her infrared flare, and electronic chaff countermeasure systems to an active state. She opened up a direct communication channel to the troops on the ground and commenced speaking, "Greenhead this is Killer Chick on-board warthog. Please respond."

After a short delay the radio replied, "Killer Chick this is Greenhead. What can we do for the lady with the painted fingernails sitting in air-conditioned comfort, still smelling all pretty from this morning's bath?"

Kelly rolled her eyes and immediately replied, "Greenhead or was that Dickhead? I've had my morning absolutely screwed coming out here to hold your hand. It's rather obvious you have time to spare down there. If anyone starts to cause you concern, I would be happy to offer my assistance. Would you acknowledge when you have a visual on me. I'm currently descending on your position from the north approximately seven miles out, over."

The radio started up with Greenhead's reply, "That's an affirmative Killer Chick we have you in sight. Come down so we can get a good look at your legs."

Kelly again rolled her eyes while throttling back still further and slowed so that she needed to deploy her flaps and slots to maintain altitude. She was now only some three hundred feet above and one and a half miles short of Greenhead's reported position. As the lift increased, she throttled up to sixty percent to maintain level flight. At such a low airspeed, the landing gear warning alarm sounded which Kelly ignored other than to mentally acknowledge she was travelling as slow as she possibly could. Kelly spoke into the radio, "Well howdy-do Greenhead. I have a visual on your position. Wave so I can tell mum all about the new man in my life, and now we know each other intimately, you can drop the formality and call me Killer."

Kelly noticed one of the soldiers stand up, take his hat off and wave it over his head. Clearly, she had found Greenhead. However, she also noticed on her GPS map display the friendly-fire lock was actually some three hundred and fifty feet from where she observed their physical position. Kelly immediately opened communications with the AWACS to inform Widow of the problem. "Widow, this is Killer. I have a visual on Greenhead. Their plotted position is displaying incorrectly on my systems. May we calibrate? Over."

Wendy responded, "That is an affirmative, Killer proceed, on your mark."

Kelly throttled up while retracting her flaps and slots and watched as her airspeed rapidly increased to three hundred and forty knots. She banked sharply left, turning around to make another pass over the troops on the ground. Opening her voice channel, she said, "Greenhead, we have a little administrative work to do up here. I will be making a low pass over your position, at speed. Please instruct your people to remain low, and I would appreciate it if they didn't shoot or throw anything in the air."

Greenhead, while sounding somewhat puzzled, acknowledged in time to see Kelly flying straight at him. As it became uncomfortably close the plane flipped over to fly inverted yet continuing to dive further downward until within a few feet of the ground, Greenhead hit the deck obviously screaming a few quickly chosen expletives. He appeared to believe the plane was about to crash and must have hoped it might make it over the top of his troops before exploding into pieces.

As Kelly passed over his position, she called into the radio, "Mark" and watched as her instruments immediately updated to display the correct location of the troops. Kelly returned herself to an upright position and proceeded to slow down and climb away from the ground to a position out of harm's way. Kelly beamed as she called Greenhead. "Hey, Greenhead, I didn't really get to look at your face. You seemed rather busy. Your butt looked fine to me. Hope the dirt tasted okay."

After a short delay, Greenhead replied with a hint of agitation in his voice, "Jesus woman, err... Killer, I hope that worked for you because from down here we missed the funny part." After another brief delay, he added, "But I'll give it to you Killer, you sure do know how to drive that thing. I take it it's not your first time this side of the barbed wire. If you don't mind, we will pass on the instant replays."

Kelly again spoke down the voice channel, "Greenhead, doesn't appear to be much excitement down there. I think I'll put on the sunglasses and take the fifty-dollar tour to check out the sights. If things get warm feel free to buzz me. Our aim is to please. I'll be around. Killer out."

Kelly climbed out of the valley into the clear above the mountains, where she could see for miles in every direction and started to take in the area for likely positions that might cause grief to the guys on the ground. There were a few huts high up in the valley. They had the potential to make a rather efficient observation post for anyone hostile with radio equipment, a phone or something to communicate firing instructions. However this would be unlikely to happen, as Kelly knew airborne command's AWACS was detecting, listening to and locating all electronic communication coming from the area. Anything hostile and they would target the position for an instant make over. The road up the valley into Pakistan was the obvious source of an intense attack. Anywhere on the surrounding hills would make for a good strike and run attack, although the lack of cover would make a repeat performance unlikely as the AWACS would automatically target any hostile fire source, and Kelly knew she would be onto the location before they were able to leave the area.

Kelly turned her attention to fuel. She did her sums, calculating she could remain here until eleven o'clock and still make it back to Bagram without drama. She noted the time was now nine-twenty, giving her ninety minutes in the area without Widow's tanker, assuming the tanker was only ten minutes in and out.

There are some things a girl must take care of herself. Fuel first before we extend our stay. So it's a tanker by eleven or I'm out of here, she told herself as she changed direction to head north towards Sarhadd for the third time.

She was passing to the west of the town and wondering if they had running water on tap down there, when the radio offered, "Killer this is Widow. We have received a joint star report of vehicle movement in Pakistan heading towards your area. They seem somewhat suspicious. We have four vehicles, two loaded lorries and two lightly loaded pick-up-sized vehicles. A satellite pass has been requested. We will have the results in a few minutes. Should these vehicles continue towards you at their current pace, they will be in your area in approximately seventy minutes. How is your fuel state for that timeframe?"

Kelly replied, "Widow, that would be towards the end of my fuel window. Perhaps we should book an extender hook-up for say, fifty minutes. This will allow us to loiter here until around fourteen hundred hours if we need to. Hope you enjoy your silver-service lunch up there. After you go to the bathroom and freshen up! If these vehicles are hostile, it's a good bet we are being observed in this area. How is Greenhead's transportation out of here progressing?"

The radio responded, "That's an affirmative Killer. We will have our Extender in position above you ready for a hook-up in forty minutes. In the meantime try not to put yourself in visual contact with the vehicles. No need to scare them off. They'll be sure to pop up somewhere else if you don't do things properly. We have detected no communication from your locality this morning, although we did catch someone having a rather long chat at dusk yesterday while Greenhead was settling in for the night. Greenhead's chinook is in the air. Estimated time of pick-up is also forty minutes. However we have asked them to delay until we see what these vehicles are doing. The chinook will be re-fuelling on the extender immediately after you and prior to the pick up. You have a nice mental experience for lunch down there, and when we have time I'll tell you all about the bubble bath I'm going to have tomorrow morning when we land. Widow out."

Gee that was a low swipe, Kelly thought. *It's all right for some. Based in Holland. Probably living in a quaint little house with a view over the canal. With a husband looking after her kids. I wonder if Wendy knows I am sharing six showers and one washbasin with one hundred and eighty-seven other females at Bagram. God, how would she like to try and stay clean while wading for eight minutes through three-inch deep dust to a cot in a tent with a dirt floor and five snoring tent-mates. I'll bet she doesn't know what it's like to balance the merit of getting dressed for a sixteen-minute round trip in the dirt to the porcelain or a quick squat out the back, like an animal, at three in the morning... I'll bet she has a chardonnay and some strawberries while she takes her bubble bath tomorrow morning.* Kelly turned to travel east towards China for a few minutes.

After her time was up flying east, Kelly headed southwest to return towards Greenhead's position. To break the boredom, she wobbled her ailerons so the plane banked sideways and sat upright at right angles to the ground, first to the right and then the left. She used her rubbers to prevent the plane from losing altitude. After six of these *hand stands,* she rolled over and flew upside down for a minute before returning to normal flight. She told herself gymnastics was a healthy exercise. Kelly passed over Greenhead's position high above him, knowing her altitude and low throttle setting would allow her to pass unnoticed. Everything seemed quiet down there, so she turned northwest, tracking towards Karkat. After several minutes, and as she approached the town, she turned south. She started to wonder if the Afghan farmers down below had morning tea or kept working through to lunch without stopping.

Kelly flew south for three minutes and was about to change direction to travel northeast when she noticed the imprint of a large plane suddenly appearing on her locating radar above and a little to her west. *That will be the extender,* she thought as it started to display a KC-10 friendly tag identification. Further to the southwest at a lower altitude, she noticed the CH-47SD friendly imprint of the chinook and was interested to notice the helicopter was miles inside Pakistan. *Must be taking a shortcut. I wonder where they have come from.*

As expected, Wendy came over the radio. "Killer this is Widow. It's time for your ten-thirty fuel stop. The extender will come down to your current altitude and sit four miles off, to your west. The low altitude is to pick up the chinook immediately after you, so maintain a lookout for both aircraft as you approach. We have a confirmation of the vehicles. They are definitely hostile. The lorries are covered and appear to be transporting troops. Both the pick-ups are armed. The lead vehicle has a light anti-aircraft gun mounted in the rear, and the second appears to have a mortar tube mounted in it. So, we will have a job for you after you refuel. Widow out."

Kelly acknowledged the message and steered westward ahead of the extender so they would merge rapidly. In only a few minutes she sat in position behind the extender, a large Boeing DC-10 ex-passenger plane, which had been converted to a flying service station. During the approach to within a few feet of her seat, at the rear of the Extender, Kelly could see the boom operator was female. Kelly watched closely as the re-fuelling boom lowered into place just inches in front of her cockpit and noticed with some intensity the fuel levels starting to rise. In two minutes Kelly was again full of fuel and *backing* slowly away. As she steadily moved left out from behind the extender, Kelly noted the chinook moving into position to take fuel and to her surprise the army pilot flying it also looked female. *Must be ladies day.* Kelly manoeuvred a safe distance away from the other aircraft. Kelly waited until the chinook also moved back from the extender and watched as the large plane gathered speed, pulling ahead while climbing up to wherever it had come down from.

Again the radio started up with Wendy's familiar voice. "Killer, this is Widow. We might have you home in time for lunch. I'll ask you to remain undetected, but move closer to Greenhead's location in preparation for a strike. The vehicles are now some six miles from his position, and I'm expecting him to report them shortly. They are travelling approximately two hundred feet apart and making thirty miles per hour. It would be rather convenient if you could pick off both the lorries before anyone has the opportunity to deploy from them. The two smaller vehicles are more likely to want to fight, so they should be easy pickings. All the vehicles are now in Afghanistan and have been targeted, as you will now be seeing on your systems. However, we would ask you to wait until they display hostile intent or Greenhead requests your intervention before you take them out. I will shortly be patching Butch Lady in the chinook onto Greenhead's voice channel so they can commence their pick-up procedure. Good hunting Killer, Widow out"

Kelly acknowledged Widow's message and immediately headed northeast, back towards Sarhadd and commenced to reduce altitude. She started targeting the vehicles and allocating ordinance from the detail now showing on her head-up display. As she worked away on her systems she listened to the conversation on Greenhead's voice channel.

"Greenhead, this is Butch Lady on-board freight train. Please respond."

"Butch Lady, this is Greenhead. What can we do for the lady in the big green whirly bird this morning?"

"Greenhead, more the other way round, I think. I have a note here from the big preacher saying go pick up some lost souls in need of a bath, spiritual cleansing and a drink. I hope you are all packed and ready to go, as my estimated time to your location will be seven minutes. I hope you guys have a good landing pad ready, as I intend to be at your location fifteen seconds maximum. So get off your thumbs."

"Copy that, Butch. Seven minutes will comply. God, whatever happened to all the nice southern girls who know their place, speak politely and always wear two petticoats?"

"Who knows, Greenhead. They probably all work in Baton Rouge, in their daddies' millinery store. I know they all failed boot camp, so you won't be finding any around here. Get your kit together if you're coming with us. Contact me and guide me in when you have a visual. Butch out"

On you, Sister. Kelly continued to ready herself to strike. *Wish I'd known what was going down before loading up this morning. With a CBU-97 sensor fuzzed weapon on-board I would have been able to sit well above and neutralize the whole convoy in one big bang. All nice and clinical -—poor fools wouldn't have known what hit them. But life is full of compromises now they'll have to watch me give them a couple of AGM-65 mavericks for the lorries and GAU-8 cannon burst on each pickup. All from the front, so we can be sure the mavericks hit something solid and explode. Should be able to effect this in one pass if they co-operate. Then I'll turn back on them, with a steep starboard turn, so we don't point towards Greenhead. I'll target anyone I missed with a few Mk82 five hundred pounders or one CBU-87 cluster bomb. I'll let them choose which for me, at the time.*

Kelly planned her route in detail. It would be low level, up the valley towards the south. This would take her directly over Greenhead's position, again. *Poor dear,* she said to herself through a wry smile.

The voice channel started up, "Butch, this is Greenhead. I can hear you but have not yet got a visual. Hold off where you are for now, as we have company here. Out to you. Killer, this is Greenhead. We have vehicle movement on the road to the south of us coming our way. Would you take a look-see for us?"

Kelly replied, "That is a negative, Greenhead. I have been instructed to lay low until these vehicles demonstrate hostile intent. We have been watching and tracking them for some time. We are ready and in position to strike. To bring you up to speed, the lead vehicle is a pick-up with a mounted light machine gun. The second vehicle is also a pick-up, and it seems to have a mortar tube in the back. These are being followed by two covered lorries, which may be carrying troops. They are travelling approximately two hundred feet apart at thirty miles per hour. It's your call. Feel free to stir them up and bring it on."

Greenhead immediately responded, "God, I hope they're lousy shots. My mother warned me I'd be sidelined on a dusty Afghan hill if I didn't study hard at school. I should have listened to her. There seems to be no room for real men in this man's army any more. I think I need a sex change. Killer, thanks for the heads-up and support, good hunting. We will fire a few shots to get their attention, standby."

Kelly had now turned south and was commencing her run into Greenhead's valley at low altitude. She armed her mavericks and targeted the first to find the third vehicle using the electro-optical trace coming via the AWACS and was automatically set to follow that vehicle. Kelly estimated she would gain visual contact with the target from eight miles out and could dispatch this missile giving her time to target a second maverick on the other lorry and fire, five miles out. Kelly would then be free to manoeuvre herself to bring the cannon to bear on the two pick-ups. *Shame I can't target several weapons at once in this old bucket. It would make life so much easier.* She started to build up speed and set herself on what she felt would be the optimum altitude.

At fourteen miles out and travelling at three hundred and eighty knots she received a message, "Killer, this is Widow. We have detected rifle fire coming from Greenhead's position; standby."

A short delay ensued then, "Killer, the lead vehicle has stopped and is firing towards Greenhead's position. You are authorized to eliminate all targets. Good hunting."

Kelly replied, "Will comply, out."

Kelly switched her attention to Greenhead's voice channel. "Greenhead, your targets have become hostile. I'm on the case from your north and am preparing to return fire. On my command, check your fire. I don't want you grunts shooting up my rear end. Standby."

Kelly banked slightly right to follow the valley and noticed she had visual contact with Greenhead and the vehicles. Her display showed eight point six miles to target. She levelled the plane to eliminate any 'G' force that might impede missile guidance. The six-second wait for the first strike seemed like two hours, but finally the missile demonstrated it had locked on target. A plume of white smoke engulfed the left side of her cockpit for an instant; a sure receipt for a successful dispatch. Kelly immediately began to target the second maverick on the fourth vehicle, a task she completed with twelve seconds to spare. Having no reason to delay, she dispatched it and received the same smoky response. Getting back on the radio, she called Greenhead. "Greenhead, check fire. You might as well sit back on your *chairs millionaire* and watch the fireworks. Killer out."

Kelly noticed all the grunts move their heads towards her as each missile streaked past, no more than fifty feet above them. *They must make one hell of a noise.* Kelly used her rudder to hold the gun sight on the lead vehicle while also bringing the second vehicle into the same alignment. She noticed the flashing of tracer-fire from the forward vehicle stream through the air in an arc away from Greenhead towards herself and watched the first missile hit its target with devastating results. There was a flash followed by a *solid* plume, then nothing but a patch of twisted black, with debris still floating around it. As the second lorry suffered the same fate, she noticed a flash rise from the second pick-up and immediately switched her attention to warn Greenhead, but before she could speak Wendy came through the voice channel. "Greenhead. Incoming mortar round prepare to take cover. I will call *splash*. Out to you. Good shooting thus far, Killer. Keep it up. Out"

Kelly ignored any response as she was approaching her point to fire on the pickups. She gave the forward vehicle a quick burst and watched as the whole thing erupted, initially disappearing in a dust ball, then exploded in a flash of flame, which quickly become deathly black. This obscured visual contact with the second vehicle for what seemed ages. Eventually she caught a sighting through the gloom, made a quick adjustment to the aircraft attitude and fired another short burst, getting the same result on that vehicle as well.

Kelly flew across the target area then banked sharply right as planned. In mid-turn she heard Wendy's *splash* on the voice channel. She passed over what had seconds before been four vehicles and many people. Obviously there was no need to use further ordinance. No one would walk away from down there. Left and forward of Greenhead, she noticed the explosion and was relieved to see the mortar round caused no harm.

Kelly opened her voice channel. "Greenhead, I guess it's time to go home. These guys won't be bothering you or uncle Sam any more."

The radio immediately responded, "Killer, copy that. Butch, come straight in and get us. I'm becoming homesick. Jesus, Killer, remind me not to ever get dirty on you. I noted your tail address, EL207, a Louisiana belle, if I'm not mistaken. You know my momma lives over near Alexandra and would just love it if we came a calling for tea one Sunday afternoon. I can hear her now, "Do you take two sugars my dear? My goodness Bernie, where ever did you find such a cute young thing?" That's when I could tell her, "Why, Momma, she is a—"

"Butch, this is Greenhead. We have a visual on you. We are located to your northeast. Throwing smoke now. Over."

Butch replied, "I see Yellow."

Followed by Greenhead, "Come in and get us. You cute southern thing, you."

And Butch again, "Greenhead. Get your mind out of your pants. Killer, impressive work you've done here. You keep that ugly thing of yours well away from me, please."

Kelly steered away from the chinook and watched it approaching Greenhead. As the chinook slowed, the rear door commenced winding down, and the smoky dust curled around it like a large waterspout engulfing the rear rotor. The rear wheels had no sooner touched the ground than Greenhead and his team raced up the ramp, disappearing inside. The chinook immediately started skyward again, with the rear door closing.

The radio came alive yet again with Wendy's familiar voice. "That's a wrap, guys. Not a bad result all round. Killer we have plotted your return path to escort Butch and her cargo southwest until you are parallel with Jalalabad, then you can make a quick northwest dash for the waiting bathroom. The course is in your display. We have conveyed our compliments to your squadron. The ground crew will be waiting to mark your nose count with four more notches."

Kelly again acknowledged and slowly commenced to climb out of the valley, sitting off the rear and to the left of the chinook. The trip home went quickly and without incident. While they were passing to the west of Jalalabad, Kelly and Butch exchanged a few niceties over the radio before Kelly peeled off, altering her course to the northwest. Kelly had just called up Bagram control and was given clearance to land, when to her surprise the radio sounded again. "Killer this is Butch. Something I thought I should share with you before put your head down tonight. The fifteen horny grunts sitting behind me, with nothing to do and plenty going on in their minds have just voted you their favourite mystery pinup girl. You are now their official *Warrior Chick.* In the context of what these guys go through each day, it's the best compliment you will ever receive. Sweet dreams. You take care. Butch, out."

The Last Page

TODAY HAS BEEN IDENTICAL to so many, and were it not for my pending execution at one minute past midnight tonight, I might well have been overtaken with despair at the thought of spending day number four thousand three hundred and twenty-four pondering the unattainable.

My name is James Charles Hopeman. I entered the system as number 6147885 on January 5th, 1993, having been sentenced to death for the murder of Christie Elinor Pritchard, a young lady of just sixteen tender years. I have never known, seen, touched or harmed Christie Elinor Pritchard. I don't expect you to believe me. No one ever does, after all this is death row. There is no room for innocence here.

I can safely say the last eleven years, three hundred and five days have been a drag. Many of the joys taken for granted are the ultimate privilege here. Seeing the stars, watching the sun set, being hot, being cold, feeling the rain, sleeping with the light out or privacy, just closing a door would be the joy of joys.

But what of Christie Elinor Pritchard? Who was she? It all came out at *that* trial. Christie, a popular school student, had attended her Formal on the evening of May 19th 1992 then somehow finished up lying in a storm water drain on the outskirts of town. She had been raped, mutilated and strangled. Her final hours must have been hellish. The evidence was believable and to the jury conclusive. Her lifeless body had been delivered to that lonely ditch in my car. There was then a road accident, where it is said I decamped the scene and returned to my temporary bed in a motel twenty-five miles away.

The arresting officer testified to my guilt by explaining how confused, disorientated and shocked I appeared to be as the police barged into *my* motel room. At the time of my arrest, the sheriff exposed proof of my guilt. He explained while sporting an outstretched finger targeting into my chest, "You don't know! You don't know! Don't insult my intelligence, Boy! We run a peaceful community. Folks from around here don't do these things! You're going to fry, Boy!"

He was of course not totally correct. It seems life had passed the sheriff by. Frying people went out ages ago. Since 1973 we inject the condemned.

I was remanded in custody. It took two hundred and thirty-three days to have my day in court. I heard someone in the gallery comment on my guilt saying, "No innocent man is going to walk into court wearing orange overalls and shackles. This guy is a bad one. He is going to fry!"

There was some logic to his argument. Under different circumstances, I may have believed him myself.

The jury believed him. They took twenty-seven minutes, over coffee, to find me guilty. A record to this day, I'm told. *'We the jury find the defendant guilty as charged,'* is all it took to seal my future. Yet those words were nothing to compare with the outburst of scorn focused upon me from the gallery. Some fixed their stare of glass upon me while others yelled cheers and advice. The Pritchard family erupted with a joy reserved for lottery winners. I wonder to this day how they could exclude their daughter's loving memory so quickly and completely from the moment. I heard the sheriff congratulate the district attorney saying, "You got the son of a bitch. Our re-election is in the bag!"

I watched my momma's face as she fell to pieces upon hearing the sheriff's remark. It penetrated her psyche. Her form aged twenty years in an instant. Her proud Virginian upbringing was washed away in a rush of tears.

All I could think of was the effort, the struggle, the journey she had undertaken to raise me to take my place in society; to respect myself and respect others. How she had always reminded me my father, who died in Vietnam before we had the chance to meet, was watching over me.

As I was led from that court house to face *my* future, I couldn't help but wonder, reminding myself of my darling momma sitting alone on a bus, crossing a fifteen-hundred-mile barrier, her hopes and dreams crushed forever.

IT TOOK TWO YEARS TO stop sulking and telling everyone how innocent I was. The answer was always the same. "Sure," they would say. I even refused to exercise preferring to remain permanently in *my* cell then to venture into the cage in shackles.

Slowly I commenced to wonder what if? What if I hadn't stopped the night in *that* motel? What if I had completed my journey to Flagstaff, Arizona and actually started the position of cadet journalist with the local newspaper? What if I wasn't consumed by self-pity? Where would I be today?

Slowly, I began to calm, change, lift and even respect myself. It took almost three years to impress myself with my first novel *When Passion Kills.* My second, *The Farce,* took only six months. My third novel, *Onion Patch* was first to be published. It became a best-seller almost overnight. This in turn sold the first two. They were all written under my pen name, *H M Lockup.* After twelve best-selling novels the rumours about the reclusive Ms Lockup were commonplace on the gossip circuits. My personal favourite was the one explaining how she lived as a recluse in Alaska, fifty miles north of Big Delta.

My novels generated many millions of dollars in royalties. The money couldn't help my legal plight. There was no evidence remaining from the murder that could be re-investigated or challenged, nothing scientific. Even my car was sold by the county three weeks after the conviction. There being no chance of an appeal to overturn the original conviction, the best I could hope to achieve was to grovel my way into spending the rest of my life in jail and as I was already doing that it all seemed like a pointless exercise in trading away much of what remained of my dignity.

Momma was never comfortable with the wealth my novels generated. She seemed embarrassed to accept any of the money. She thought it a cruel trick that she had the means to acquire anything but could not attain the one thing she wanted most.

Just over three years ago, momma suffered a massive stroke on the bus travelling home from visiting me. She died instantly. They said she didn't suffer, but it's my guess she couldn't suffer any more. I had asked her to travel by air, but she felt more comfortable remaining nearer to the ground.

I was not permitted to attend my mother's funeral.

———— ✦ ————

THE WARDEN AND A CHAPLAIN have just entered *my* cell. They never seemed comfortable with the job at these times. The warden struggled with his request saying, "Deep down we know you can't. But, it is our duty to ask that you confess to the murder of Christie Elinor Pritchard and detail what happened on the night of her murder. The family would be able to find closure and comfort knowing why she was murdered and that you regret your actions."

I again said I had no idea what happened to Christie Elinor Pritchard, adding that in a little over thirty minutes I intended to ask her myself what happened — if the chaplain's afterlife world eventuates. I also added it was going to be a true joy talking to someone who obviously harbours no doubt as to my innocence.

The warden handed me a heart monitor and asked me to put it on under my shirt, so the doctor could do his job. I complied. The warden again wanted me to allow my solicitor to consider an approach for a stay of execution from the state governor adding, if I allowed my other identity to be revealed, he wouldn't dare permit the proceedings to continue. I rejected this. I have had enough. I also politely told the chaplain to reserve all his religious mumbo jumbo for someone who believes in his form spiritual help.

The warden struggled with emotion while wishing me well as both men left me alone with my solicitor, who was now sharing the cell. My solicitor and I discussed a number of things. He raised the issue of a plea to the governor. His eyes told me he knew full well what my response would be. We discussed my legacy and in particular the trusts I had set up. One was a generous trust to assist the children of death row inmates receive a college education. Another was to help disadvantaged prisoners gain legal assistance and also afford them the means to finish their own education.

We discussed the launch of my thirteenth novel, titled *Death Row – The Final Page,* which was to take place the following day. In particular the solicitor went though a press release he would read after tonight's proceeding had been finalized.

IT WAS TIME:

The guards escort me next door to the chamber. The warden reads a proclamation of death out loud and asks if I wish to make a final statement.

I say, "It is my hope that any members of the Pritchard family here tonight salvage the comfort they seek. Those of you who are saddened by these proceedings, please don't be concerned. I have had enough of the sameness of life. There is no more I can discover. This is my last page."

With that I climb on the bunk and expose my receptive veins to the juices of eternity.

About EA Harwik

I'm a dreamer who found an old pen.

I sometimes dream of the unattainable, imagine it might be so and turn my energy to the written word. Writing helps me feel more worthy.

THANK YOU FOR READING Tales by Erin.

EA Harwik (Erin)

eaharwik@eaharwik.com

http://www.eaharwik.com

www.ingramcontent.com/pod-product-compliance
Lightning Source LLC
Chambersburg PA
CBHW052233150726
48002CB00003B/1410